GHOST
DOG

GHOST DOG

Ellen Leroe
Illustrated by Bill Basso

HYPERION BOOKS FOR CHILDREN
New York

A Lucas • Evans Book

Text © 1993 by Ellen Leroe. Illustrations © 1993 by Bill Basso. All rights
reserved. Printed in the United States of America. For information address
Hyperion Books for Children, 114 Fifth Avenue, New York, New York 10011.

FIRST EDITION

1   3   5   7   9   10   8   6   4   2

The artwork for each picture is prepared using pencil with ink wash.
This book is set in 13-point Garamond Book.

Library of Congress Cataloging-in-Publication Data

Leroe, Ellen
 Ghost Dog/Ellen Leroe; illustrated by Bill Basso.—1st ed.
  p. cm.
 Summary: Nine-year-old Artie Jensen gets help from his new pet, Ghost
Dog, an invisible pug, after someone steals the valuable baseball card his
grandfather gave him.
 ISBN 1-56282-268-3 (trade)—ISBN 1-56282-269-1 (lib. bdg.)
 [1. Animal ghosts—Fiction. 2. Dogs—Fiction. 3. Ghosts—Fiction.
4. Baseball cards—Fiction. 5. Mystery and detective stories.]
I. Basso, Bill, ill. II. Title.
PZ7.L5614Gh   1993
[Fic]—dc20   92-72020
                                                         CIP
                                                          AC

For Gordon R. Marks,
a special part of my life
—E. L.

For Marie
—B. B.

GHOST DOG

Three strange things happened to me at the end of the summer.

Grandpa Noonie's new house turned out to be haunted, I got to play detective, and I worked on my first big case with the help of the ghost!

Maybe I better explain.

My name is Aristotle ("Artie") Jensen, and I'm nine.

The ghost is a wrinkly faced pug poltergeist with a nose for detection. Since I don't know his real name, I call him Ghost Dog. He seems to like it. Ghost Dog doesn't talk—he barks—but I can understand him.

We're an unusual pair, but together we solved our first case: the Mystery of the Stolen Rookie Baseball Card. Maybe you heard or read about it. It was in all the newspapers and even on TV. Really major league stuff! And it started Labor Day weekend when my mom and two-year-old baby sister, Sarah, and I piled into the car and drove to Grandpa Noonie's new house. Grandpa Noonan, whom everyone calls Noonie, had just moved into a big old place in a small town near Philadelphia. It's two hours from where we live, and my favorite aunt and uncle—Aunt Min and Uncle Bob—and my *un*favorite cousins, Homer and Socko, live practically right across the street.

We got there late Friday afternoon. Grandpa Noonie hurried out of the house and down the steps as soon as he heard us pull in. He was wearing a funny rubber nose that made him look like a pig.

"Oink, oink, oink, oink!" Grandpa Noonie squealed.

Then he held out his arms and hugged us all. The rubber nose tickled.

Sarah and I laughed. My mother rolled her eyes and groaned.

"You're just like a big kid, Dad!"

He took off the nose and put it on my mother, and she laughed, too.

Just then my two cousins rode up on their bikes. Homer was 10 and into Little League baseball and doing local TV commercials. Socko was 13 and went on and on about skateboarding and his baseball card club. I loved baseball, too, but you'd never get my older cousins to play with me. I was a baby in their eyes.

Now I picked up my mom's heaviest suitcase to show them how tough I was.

"Hey, it's Artie Schwarzenegger," Homer said with a laugh.

"Sure you don't need help with that?" Socko added, winking at his brother.

My legs felt like rubber and my face turned

bright red, but I made it to the front door.

"See you at dinner tonight, Biceps Man," Homer called out. "If you get your breath back!"

Laughing together, my two cousins rode off. I stared after them, making my fiercest dinosaur face. I may be only nine-year-old Artie Jensen, but secretly I'm also hero of my own made-up comic book, The Adventures of Dino Boy. Half-boy/half-dinosaur, I'm able to squash entire schools flat with one whack of my gigantic tyrannosaurus-shaped tail. Or scare "think-they-know-everything" cousins with my long, pointed teeth and dangerous roar.

Grandpa Noonie hurried up the walk and took the bag from me. He helped us carry the rest of the suitcases inside.

"Want to take a tour of the new house?" he asked. "I bet Aristotle here would like to see my newest video games. I just got Lazer Blazer."

Grandpa Noonie loves video games. Sometimes he starts playing and doesn't stop until it's time for dinner.

"Can I play Lazer Blazer now?" I asked.

My mother shook her head. "Later. Let Grandpa take you on a tour of the house, and then he'll show you your room. I want you to unpack and keep Sarah out of my hair while I start dinner."

Grandpa Noonie showed Sarah and me the house, then took us to a room on the second floor.

"Your bedroom for the weekend," he said, and put my overnight bag on the small bed in the corner. "It's nothing fancy, but there's a TV set."

"Great," I said. "I want to catch some of the Phillies game."

Sarah tugged at my grandfather's leg. "Cookies?"

Grandpa Noonie went down to the kitchen and came back with fruit juice, a bag of potato chips, and some raisin cookies.

"This should keep you until dinner," he said, and left to talk to my mom.

Sarah quickly grabbed the cookies. I turned on the TV to the baseball game and began to

14

unpack. I took my dinosaur collection from the suitcase and lined the animals up on the dressing table so they could watch the game.

Someone hit a homer. I jumped on the bed and swung my own imaginary bat.

"I am Dino Boy, pride of the Brontosaurus Braves! Watch me drive that ball clear out of the park! Now we lead going into the eighth inning, and it's all because of that humdinger homer!"

I turned my back for a second and the game suddenly went off.

"Sarah!" I yelled, crashing back to earth in a second as plain old Artie Jensen. "You quit changing channels on me!"

But when I turned around, my sister wasn't near the remote. Or even close to the set.

And then I saw the bag of potato chips fly up in the air and turn upside down. Chips flew everywhere but mysteriously disappeared before they could land!

My mouth fell open. I froze like a statue.

But when the can of fruit juice slid along the

dresser without anyone touching it, I came to life. I grabbed up Sarah from the floor and yanked open the door. I ran down the steps, screaming, "Mom! Grandpa Noonie! This house is haunted!"

I raced back up the stairs two at a time with my mother and grandfather behind me. Sarah was still wiggling in my arms.

"Now you'll see what I'm talking about," I said as we burst into the room.

A weird glowing shape about two feet high stood in front of the bed. I blinked my eyes, but it didn't go away.

"It's a dog, for pete's sake!" I yelled. "A short, fat, little wrinkly faced pug! It's eating all the potato chips! Now do you believe me?"

17

My mother took a step forward and stared into every corner of the room. "Is this your idea of a joke, young man? Dragging us all up here for nothing!"

My mouth dropped open. "You mean you don't see it? Come on, Mom, it's right there! An ugly little dog with potato chip crumbs all over his face!"

The dog growled. It sat back and opened its mouth and let out a howl. Maybe it didn't like me calling it ugly.

"You can't tell me that you don't hear *that*!" I turned to Grandpa Noonie. "You hear it barking, don't you! You can see it, can't you?"

But Grandpa Noonie just let out a chuckle and shook his head. "You've got some imagination, Aristotle! A potato-chip-eating pug dog, who just happens to be invisible! That's really clever!"

My mother frowned. "It's not so clever, Dad. Your grandson here has been begging us to get a dog for a pet. That's all we've heard for the last month or so. First it was dinosaurs, then it

was baseball stars, now it's dogs! Honestly, Art, you're carrying this too far!"

The pug wrestled with the empty potato chip bag, making it slide and rustle across the wooden floor.

"Look, Mom! Look! It's moving the bag!"

Grandpa Noonie glanced down at the twitching potato chip bag, then across the room. He looked at me with a twinkle in his eyes.

"Maybe your pug is doing it, Aristotle, but then again, maybe the wind from the open window is making the bag move. What do you think?"

I stared—no, glared—at the pug. I gave him a scowl.

He quit playing with the potato chip bag and scowled right back at me!

I couldn't believe no one else saw him.

"But Mom, Grandpa Noonie, he's right there! He's really there!"

My mother crossed her arms and gave me a stern look.

"Nice try, Aristotle Jensen, but no go. Your

little joke is not going to make me buy you a dog."

"But Mom . . . !"

"I said no. Now fun and games are over. Aunt Min just called. She and the boys are coming over for dinner, so I want you to get out of that dirty T-shirt and into a clean shirt. And no more talk about dogs, real or imagined!"

And with a shake of her head, my mother turned and left the room. My grandfather was about to follow, but then he leaned down to whisper in my ear. "I've got something for you that's going to make you forget all about your invisible friend. So cheer up!"

"A surprise?"

"A big surprise," Grandpa Noonie promised with a grin. "Better than a ghost any day!"

When he left, I turned to face the poltergeist pug, but he had disappeared. I scratched my head. Had I been imagining it all?

Sarah ran into the room and patted the spot where our uninvited visitor had been.

"Doggie?" she said with a question in her voice. "Where's nice doggie?"

He was a doggie, all right, but he was also a ghost. A ghost dog. And until I could think up a better name, Ghost Dog was what I'd call him.

Talk about a weird weekend. It was turning out to be even more colorful than a made-up Dino Boy adventure!

Grandpa Noonie had promised me a surprise.
I waited for it all through dinner.

I waited for it all through dessert.

Aunt Min and Uncle Bob talked to my mom and Grandpa Noonie nonstop, while Homer and Socko just kept eating brownie after brownie. Homer eyed my untouched dessert plate and gave me a smirk.

"You want to pick up heavy suitcases, you need to put more weight on that lean machine of yours."

I grew twenty feet in my chair to become the incredibly muscular Dino Boy, strongest creature on the planet. I stared at my cousin and felt my teeth grow as long and as pointy as sharpened pencils. I didn't even open my mouth. My tyrannosaurus teeth would give me away.

"You're awfully quiet tonight, Artie," Uncle Bob said with a smile.

I mumbled something and looked over at Grandpa Noonie. He knew why I hadn't done much talking that evening.

He knew that I was think, think, thinking about the surprise.

And anyway, even if I wanted to, I couldn't get a word in edgewise with everyone talking.

"There he goes again," Socko said on my right, poking me in the side. "Clamming up on us."

I wished that just once I could poke Socko back, but he was four years older, five inches taller, and maybe thirty pounds heavier.

But Dino Boy could let out a bellow and roar

and pick Socko up between his tyrannosaurus-shaped teeth and really give him a good shaking.

I tried to make my eyes narrow into ferocious, man-eating Dino Boy slits as I picked up one of the brownies Aunt Min had baked.

Across the table Homer giggled. "Why's Artie gone all cross-eyed on us? He looks silly."

Silly. My two older cousins always treated me like a baby.

And then, to make matters worse, I felt a tug at my knee. I looked down to see Ghost Dog looking up at me and panting. There was a weird expression on his funny face. I think he was staring at the chocolate brownie in my hand.

"Go away!" I snapped. "Get lost!"

"Why, Aristotle Jensen, how dare you talk to your cousins that way!" my mother demanded in a horrified voice. "They were just teasing you."

Homer and Socko stared at me with rounded eyes.

"You apologize at once!" my mother ordered.

"But I didn't say it to them. I said it to Ghost

Dog! He's right under the table."

"Ghost Dog?" Aunt Min asked.

"Ghost Dog?" Uncle Bob repeated, eyebrows twitching.

"Ghost Dog?" Homer and Socko yelled at the same time. They looked at each other and then over at me as if I were crazy.

"Not Ghost Dog again," my mother said. She put her knife and fork down with a thump.

"But who, or *what*, is Ghost Dog?" Uncle Bob demanded. He and everyone around the table stopped eating dessert and stared at me.

"Doggie," Sarah hummed in her baby voice. "Nice doggie!"

"Just another imaginary playmate of Aristotle's," my mother explained. "He thinks we'll get him a real dog if he drives us crazy with this invisible one."

"Maybe you will," Grandpa Noonie said with a friendly wink across the table at me.

I smiled back, but then Ghost Dog started barking. He wanted dessert, and it happened to be the plate of chocolate brownies close to the edge of the table. I shook my head and frowned at him, but he didn't listen. Before I could do anything, the junk-food-loving pug gripped the table cloth and gave it a good yank.

Dishes clattered. Silverware rattled. Glasses shivered. The chocolate brownies slid off the table and onto the floor. Ghost Dog yelped happily and sat down to munch his dessert.

"Aristotle, you go to your room at once," my mother ordered, rearranging the dishes. "I cannot believe what a mess you've made, showing off like that in front of your cousins and aunt and uncle."

I jumped to my feet. "But, Mom, I didn't do it! I swear it! It was Ghost Dog!"

"Ghost Dog! If I hear that name one more time . . ." She stood up with a frown and pointed to the door.

No use arguing with that frown. I stomped out of the room and up to the second floor. I knocked my dinosaurs over.

I had gotten yelled at by my mother in front of my cousins and been made to look like a baby.

I had missed out on my grandfather's surprise.

Now I'd probably never find out what he'd been planning to show me.

The weekend was turning into a disaster, and it was all Ghost Dog's fault.

Things went from terrible to terrific the very next day.

Mom had gotten over being angry with me, I didn't bump into Ghost Dog at all, and Grandpa gave me the surprise.

He had bought me a ticket to my very first baseball card show!

"You can't miss it," Grandpa Noonie said as he handed me the ticket. "It's being held four blocks from the house, at the town hall right smack dab in the center of town."

I read the names on the ticket in awe. "Mickey Mantle's going to be there signing autographs! And so's Jose Canseco and Roger Clemens! I can't believe it!"

Grandpa Noonie chuckled and ruffled my hair. "Figured you'd enjoy seeing your heroes, kiddo. And Uncle Bob and Homer are going, too. They'll have to meet you there because Homer's got baseball practice this morning."

"Great!"

"Oh, one more thing before I forget. The last part of the surprise."

My grandfather pulled something out of his pocket and motioned for me to come closer. He opened his hand, and I stared at a baseball card of the New York Mets pitcher Tom Seaver.

I had a more recent card of Tom Seaver myself, from his last season in the major leagues, but Grandpa Noonie assured me his was special.

"You see the date on this, Aristotle? It's 1967. Seaver was starting out then, a rookie. The card cost me almost nothing back then. Seaver's in the Hall of Fame now, and I think you can get

31

close to a hundred dollars for a rookie card like this. Take it to the show today and sell it. Then buy something for yourself that you'd really like."

"Hey, thanks, Grandpa Noonie!" I took the rookie card and put it in my pocket along with the ticket. I had my grandfather's one-hundred-dollar baseball card to protect. I became Dino

Boy, out to guard the Seaver card while sneaking my way through a jungle full of spies, danger, and quicksand.

I got no farther than a block when I sensed someone was following me. I felt eyes burning into the back of my shirt. I swore I heard footsteps behind me. But when I turned around, no one was there. It gave me a creepy feeling until I heard barking. I'd recognize that bark anywhere.

Sure enough, Ghost Dog appeared on the sidewalk.

I stopped and gave him a dirty look. "Haven't you caused enough trouble already? I don't need you following me, ruining my day. So beat it."

The funny-faced pug just stood there, wagging that curly little tail.

"I said, beat it! Scram! Get lost!"

He refused to disappear. I grunted something but decided to keep walking. I wasn't going to let Ghost Dog ruin an otherwise great day.

One block from the town hall, I saw Socko's

fancy bike parked outside a comic book and card shop called the Strike Zone. I peeked in the door and saw my older cousin talking and laughing with his friends, probably the members of his baseball card club. Then I got an idea. What if I showed them the Seaver rookie card? They'd be impressed, and then I wouldn't look like such a baby to Socko.

Keep on walking, Dino Boy, I told myself. Forget the idea. Your mission is to get Grandpa Noonie's card to the baseball card show safely.

But the look on Socko's know-it-all face would be priceless. I'd have the last laugh for once. I couldn't help myself.

I took one step inside the shop and felt my leg being yanked in the opposite direction. Ghost Dog was trying to stop me, as if he sensed danger in my little plan.

"Let go!" I muttered. "Stop that! I know what I'm doing!"

I half-walked, half-dragged myself inside the busy Strike Zone, Ghost Dog pulling at my leg with all his strength.

The store was crowded, but Socko saw me.

"What are you doing here?"

I made myself stand up taller, try to look older. "I think I have a valuable card," I announced in a loud voice.

As casually as I could, I pulled the Tom Seaver card out of my pocket and held it up for the store owner to see. Socko stared at the card and shrugged. "Doesn't look valuable to me," he said. "In fact, I've got two Seaver cards, so what's the big deal with this one?"

His friends laughed. My face turned bright red, but the store owner grabbed the card and then shook his head at my cousin.

"The kid is right," he said. "He's got himself a hot card. A '67 rookie Seaver card has become worth about one thousand dollars."

I hurriedly took the card back from the store owner.

"A thousand dollars?" Socko's eyes widened in shock. People around me began asking questions, trying to see the card in my hand. My cousin and his friends were pushed against the

counter by everyone crowded around me. I started to feel trapped. I started to feel frightened. I wished that I had listened to Ghost Dog after all.

I was going to lose the card because I wanted to show off, and it was all my fault.

Someone came to the rescue.

Big, strong arms picked me up and carried me out of the store. When I was set down, I turned to find a tall, muscular man with dark, curly hair grinning at me.

"Hey, are you all right?" he asked. "I didn't want you to get smothered by that mob in there."

"No, I-I'm fine, I think. Thanks." I smiled back at him in relief when I realized I still had the card in my hand. Grandpa's thousand-dollar card!

Beside me Ghost Dog had reappeared and was acting funny. He stood at attention, body rigid, baring his teeth and growling at the stranger. Seeing him act this way scared me. He really looked ferocious!

But then I forgot all about the ugly little pug when I heard what the man was saying. His name was Gary Wilsen, and he was a reporter for the local paper. He was covering the baseball card show today, and he wanted to do an article about me and the card!

"Think about it," he said. "Your picture will be in the newspaper. Right on the very front page. Headline news. Your family will be so proud."

His voice was soft and hypnotic. I didn't understand why owning the rookie card would land me in the newspaper, but Gary Wilsen was a reporter, and I believed him. I really wanted to see my face on the front page. And Homer and Socko would point to it and cry, "Hey, there's our famous cousin, Aristotle! Is it too late to ask him to join our baseball card club? Join it? Heck, he's got to be president!"

It all sounded perfect except that Ghost Dog was baring his teeth at this reporter and making serious attack noises. If I didn't know better, I'd say that Ghost Dog was trying to defend me against possible danger.

But what possible danger was there in a harmless newspaper article?

Before I realized what I was doing, I heard myself saying "All right. What do I have to do?"

The reporter smiled. "Nothing too difficult. Let me check with my editor first about the story. Once I get his go-ahead, I can do the interview and take a picture of you holding the card."

"Great!"

"There's only one problem. The editor may not believe that you really own such an unusual baseball card. Unless I can prove it to him. But how?" Gary Wilsen thought a minute, frowning.

Then he snapped his fingers. "I've got it! We need to go to the editor together, and you can show him the card."

Ghost Dog was tugging at my jeans, trying to pull me away from Gary Wilsen. But Gary Wilsen wasn't the one who had gotten me into trouble before. It was Ghost Dog. Of the two of them, I trusted the reporter more. Besides, I wanted to tell my cousins I visited the local paper and talked to the editor.

"It won't take long," the reporter promised. He turned and pointed across the street. "See, the newspaper offices are in that building. We can be in and out in less than five minutes."

Motioning for Ghost Dog to be quiet, I followed the reporter across the street and into the small but noisy newspaper office. Gary Wilsen left me on the worn sofa waiting while he talked to the receptionist in low tones.

"Can I see the card for a minute?" Gary Wilsen said, coming over to me.

I handed it over, and he flashed me a grin.

"The boss is in a big meeting, so I need you

41

to wait out here while I go in the back to show him the card."

"Wait out here?" I asked a little suspiciously.

"Only for a minute; I promise. I'll have you meet the editor as soon as I pull him out of this meeting."

I nodded and sat on the sofa. Gary Wilsen hurried down a hallway and disappeared from view. I waited, feeling excited but also a little nervous.

"I bet I get my picture in the paper," I bragged to Ghost Dog. "And here you are so worried."

There was no answering bark. I looked down, but Ghost Dog wasn't anywhere in sight.

Ghost Dog had disappeared.

Five minutes passed.

Gary Wilsen did not appear.

Six minutes.

No sign.

I began to kick the sofa. I went up to the woman at the reception desk who was working on a word processor, and I took a deep breath.

"Excuse me," I said, "can you find out how much longer Gary Wilsen is going to be?"

The woman blinked at me, but kept typing. "Gary Wilsen?"

"He's a reporter. He works here." My stomach tightened when the woman shook her head.

"I'm sorry, but I don't know any Gary Wilsen, and I know all the reporters who work here. There is a Gertrude Willnut, though. She's assistant sports editor."

My heart began pounding. My hands began to shake. "But . . . but that man who just talked to you before and walked through to the back. He told me he was Gary Wilsen and he worked here!"

The receptionist stopped typing. "Well, he never gave me his name. He said he was here to place an ad, so I sent him along to the classified section. Hey, you don't look so good. Is anything wrong?"

Wrong? Not much—except Grandpa Noonie's rookie Seaver card had been stolen. I had to find the man who took the card!

I started to race out of the office when I heard a familiar sound. Ghost Dog was back, and he was barking up a storm. Before I could open the front door, he jumped right through the wood into my arms.

"Ghost Dog!" I cried.

I have to admit I was happy to see him.

He leaped out of my arms and began jumping up and down and tugging at my leg. He pulled me out the door and along the sidewalk until I grabbed a parking meter and held on.

"Slow down a minute," I said. "What's going on? Where have you been?"

He stopped tugging and gave me the strangest look. The kind of look that said he knew exactly what had happened and stop asking stupid questions and just follow.

"Okay, boy," I said. "Show me."

Ghost Dog led me two blocks down and across the street to the town hall.

"Wait a minute," I said. "What are we doing here, for pete's sake? Why—?"

Quick-witted, super-intelligent Dino Boy would have understood in a flash, but plain old nine-year-old Artie Jensen had to put two and two together. I finally got it. The thief had come to the baseball card show to sell the Seaver card.

"We've got to get inside and stop him before it's too late!"

Ghost Dog barked in agreement. I pulled out my ticket. Once inside, I stared in shock at the large jam-packed room. Every square foot was filled with booths, exhibits, excited fans, and card collectors. How was I ever going to locate the thief?

But then I realized I had the best detective in the world with me. Even better than Dino Boy. Ghost Dog knew Gary Wilsen's scent. He could find him in this crowd faster than I could.

"Go on," I urged the pug. "Do your stuff."

Ghost Dog barked a few times, then bent his head and began to use his powerful sense of smell. Black nose twitching, he raced from one spot to another. I ran along with him, crashing blindly into people and display booths.

"Hey, watch out!" people yelled.

Would Ghost Dog save the day? Would he find the thief? He was zigzagging all over but couldn't seem to locate the man who called himself Gary Wilsen.

I was just beginning to give up when Ghost Dog zeroed in on an unusually large crowd of

people at a booth and began to bark wildly. I hurried over.

"Are you sure our man is in there?" I whispered. "I can't see him!"

Ghost Dog grabbed hold of my pants and yanked me into the crowd. Little by little I inched in closer and then, bingo! I heard people talking about a Seaver rookie card. And sure enough, when I jumped up and down for a better look, I could see the dark, curly head of the thief. He was showing the card to a dealer. But how in the world could I get close enough to the man? I was jammed in at belt-level to maybe thirty grown-ups.

Ghost Dog came to the rescue.

Being invisible he simply flew through the crowd to the front of the dealer's table. I couldn't see what was happening, but I heard a man cry out, "Something bit me!" And then the mob went crazy.

"It's gone!" someone screamed. "The card's been stolen."

"Call security!" someone else cried.

The next thing I saw was Ghost Dog hurtling back to me with the baseball card gripped between his teeth. I cheered and took it out of Ghost Dog's mouth.

"Good going!" I praised the pug. "You're the best dog anyone's ever had! Now let's get out of here!"

We turned and ran . . . straight into the arms of two big security guards.

And then Gary Wilsen appeared and pointed at me.

"There's the thief!" he cried. "That kid just stole my card!"

’m no thief!” I cried. “It’s my card!”

One of the guards held on to me gently but firmly. The other took the card out of my hand. He gave me a doubting frown.

“I mean it!” I said. I pointed to Gary Wilsen. “He’s the one who stole the card! He stole it from me inside the newspaper office not more than ten or fifteen minutes ago.”

The curly haired man snorted. “Newspaper office! The kid’s lying. Did you get a good look at that card in your hands, officers? It’s an in-

expensive card of Seaver, priced at two to three dollars. Why would I want to steal a card that's worth so little?"

"My grandfather gave me the card," I said. "And he told me it's worth a hundred dollars because it's a rookie card from 1967 and Tom Seaver's now in the Hall of Fame. A card dealer told me it was worth a thousand dollars."

The guards exchanged looks. One scratched his head. "We should hold both the man and the boy until we find out who's telling the truth."

Gary Wilsen's eyes flashed. His face turned bright red. "Are you telling me you actually believe that—that lying little brat? He stole my card, and now he's making up a crazy story about its being worth a thousand dollars. And don't forget, he bit me!" He waved his hand around.

"All right, sir, calm down," one of the guards said. "If you could step to the office in back so we can phone this boy's grandfather, we'll try to straighten this out."

"I can prove right now that the card is mine," stated Gary Wilsen. "I have certain identifying marks on the card that I can show you, if you'll let me have the card for a moment."

The guard hesitated, then handed the card over.

Gary Wilsen grabbed it and immediately turned on his heel and ran.

"Hey!" the guard yelled. "You come back with the evidence!"

"Let's get him!" cried the other.

I stood there for a second, too surprised to move. But then Ghost Dog took off, and I had to follow.

Gary Wilsen was smart. Instead of making for the heavily guarded exit at the back of the hall, he headed for the two long lines of fans waiting to get autographs from Mickey Mantle and Jose Canseco. The lines were so long they snaked around various tables. In seconds the man disappeared when he broke through one of the lines.

"We're going to lose him," one of the guards

yelled. "He can slip out the side exit!"

The two guards tried to push past the crowds to get to the thief, but the crowds pushed back. The man was going to escape with Grandpa Noonie's baseball card after all, and there was nothing I could do to stop it!

But Ghost Dog raced into action. He took off after the thief with incredible ease, melting right through the crowds.

"Go, Ghost Dog!" I cried. "Get him!"

The invisible pug didn't act like he heard me, but everyone else around me did. They turned and stared, but I didn't stick around long enough to let it bother me. I wanted to catch up with Ghost Dog. I pushed through the autograph lines and spotted Gary Wilsen. He was in front of me, heading for the side door. In all the confusion, no one was stopping him. The guards were far behind, and I still had a way to go. He was going to escape.

"Ghost Dog!" I shouted. "Do something!"

Just as the thief reached the door, I saw Ghost Dog tip over a large box behind Mickey Mantle's

chair. Baseballs spilled out and rolled right into the path of Gary Wilsen.

Gary Wilsen threw up his hands and started dancing over the rolling balls. As he lost his balance and came crashing down, he dropped the baseball card. Before it could hit the ground, Ghost Dog snapped up the card. I raced over at that moment, and Ghost Dog neatly dropped it into my outstretched hands.

Then I lost my balance and fell.

The crowd standing in line went wild, clapping and laughing.

I must have looked silly. But it didn't matter. I had Grandpa Noonie's valuable rookie card. And the guards had surrounded an angry Gary Wilsen.

Ghost Dog padded up and licked my face. Then the crowd stopped laughing and became really quiet. I blinked and looked up into the smiling faces of Mickey Mantle and Jose Canseco.

"Nice catch, kid!" said Jose Canseco.

"Can I have your autograph?" teased Mickey Mantle.

I was a hero.

Kind of. That is, after my mother finished giving me a good talking-to.

Since no one knew about Ghost Dog, they all thought I had tracked down the thief myself. But I could never have gotten back Grandpa Noonie's baseball card without the help of Ghost Dog. Dino Boy was good, but together with Ghost Dog, we made an unbeatable team.

All day Saturday I had to tell my story over

and over: to the police, to the people at the baseball card show, to Grandpa Noonie, to my family, and to reporters from the paper. Homer and Socko still could not believe that Jose Canseco and Mickey Mantle had talked to me and given me an autographed bat and baseball to take home. My cousins asked me lots of questions and didn't once treat me like a baby.

On Sunday after breakfast Grandpa Noonie opened up the newspaper and let out a cry.

"Hey, everyone, come look! Guess who's on the front page!"

My mother hurried over with Sarah and let out a gasp. "Why, Aristotle Jensen, I cannot believe it!"

But there I was, in black and white, standing between Mickey Mantle and Jose Canseco at the baseball card show. The grin on my face stretched as wide as the baseball bat I was holding. The caption above the article read: Nine-Year-Old Detective Nabs Baseball Card Thief. We found out that Gary Wilsen was wanted by the police for burglary and was now safely back in jail. I bet he felt funny stealing a card he claimed was worth only two dollars!

Later on we had a picnic at the park. Grandpa Noonie and I grilled hot dogs and hamburgers, but every time I turned my back, Ghost Dog would jump up and steal the food.

"Bad dog!" I said, but I wasn't really mad.

How could I be annoyed with such a great dog?

After lunch Socko pulled out ball and bat and gloves.

"What do you say, Art," he said, "want to play?"

Ghost Dog and I ran onto the field. Grandpa Noonie played shortstop, Homer was pitcher, and Socko went up to bat.

Socko swung and missed, swung and missed. Then the ball connected with the bat with a mighty crack and soared high in the air. It was heading right my way!

My heart began thumping. My glove felt slippery.

Here it came, a white dot getting closer and closer. And bigger and bigger.

"Get it, Aristotle!" Grandpa Noonie yelled.

I wanted to. But my feet were frozen. I was too scared to move.

And then Ghost Dog made this incredible five foot jump. He leaped into the air and caught the ball in his mouth before it beaned me on the head, then he wiggled the ball right into my motionless outstretched glove.

My family went crazy. Grandpa Noonie cheered, and so did my mother and Sarah, who both ran out onto the field. Socko and Homer stood there with shocked expressions on their faces, their mouths hanging open.

"That's the best catch I've ever seen!" Grandpa Noonie called to me. "Now come on in for some dessert!"

"I owe you, Ghost Dog," I said. I grinned at him, and he grinned right back. Together we raced to the picnic tables, Sarah at our heels.

On Monday afternoon we packed to leave. Grandpa Noonie came into my room and picked up the rookie Seaver card on the bed.

"How come you didn't sell this card at the show, Artie? You told me lots of people there wanted to buy it."

I smiled at my grandfather. "The card got me onto the front page of the newspaper and Homer and Socko played baseball with me. I'm never going to sell my Tom Seaver rookie card or trade it."

"Then I'm glad I gave it to you," Grandpa Noonie said. He gave me a big hug, and I hugged him back.

Before long it was time to go. My grandfather helped load the car, and then he and Sarah sat on the front porch while my mother called my father to tell him we were leaving. While everyone was busy I rushed around trying to find Ghost Dog.

I hadn't seen him all day.

Saying good-bye to that funny-faced, potato-chip-eating pug was going to be hard, but I still wanted to do it. I looked high and low. I couldn't find him.

"Aristotle, let's go!" my mother called. I had to stop searching.

I helped buckle Sarah in her special car seat in the back, then got in next to her. I was feeling so down I didn't want my mother to see my face.

Grandpa Noonie put on his rubber pig nose and waved to us as we pulled out, but I wasn't smiling this time. Mom honked, and we waved.

I stared out the window but didn't see anything. I pulled out my toy dinosaurs but I didn't feel like Dino Boy. My heart wasn't in it.

Suddenly I felt a warm, wet nose against my hand.

I saw my dinosaur turn upside down in mid-air.

I heard the familiar sound of barking.

And then Ghost Dog popped up in the backseat! I was so happy I dropped all the dinosaurs and let out a yell.

"Artie, is everything all right back there?" my mother asked.

"It's fine, Mom. No, it's great! It couldn't be better!"

With Ghost Dog beside me, I just knew I'd be in for plenty more adventures!